P9-DCR-708

Riley Park

Riley Park

Diane Tullson

orca soundings

ORCA BOOK PUBLISHERS

Library and Archives Canada Cataloguing in Publication

Tullson, Diane, 1958-
Riley Park / written by Diane Tullson.

(Orca soundings)
ISBN 978-1-55469-124-1 (bound).--ISBN 978-1-55469-123-4 (pbk.)

I. Title. II. Series.

PS8589.U6055R54 2009   jC813'.6   C2008-908112-9

Summary: The victim of a vicious assault, seventeen-year-old Corbin
struggles to get his life back and deal with the loss of his best friend.

First published in the United States, 2009
Library of Congress Control Number: 2008943407

Orca Book Publishers gratefully acknowledges the support for its publishing
programs provided by the following agencies: the Government of Canada
through the Book Publishing Industry Development Program and the Canada
Council for the Arts, and the Province of British Columbia through the BC
Arts Council and the Book Publishing Tax Credit.

Cover design by Teresa Bubela
Cover photography by Getty Images

ORCA BOOK PUBLISHERS
PO Box 5626, STN. B
VICTORIA, BC CANADA
V8R 6S4

ORCA BOOK PUBLISHERS
PO Box 468
CUSTER, WA USA
98240-0468

www.orcabook.com
Printed and bound in Canada.
Printed on 100% PCW recycled paper.
12 11 10 09 • 5 4 3 2 1

For Cathy, with love.

Thanks to writers Shelley, Kim, Maggie, Luke, Laura, Mollie, Rebekah, Dan, Kara, Adam, Erin, Kari, Brie and Brandy, and to Andrew, always.

Chapter One

In the Safeway parking lot, I drop two flats of beer into the back of my car. I leave the hatch open and wait for Darius to arrive with the hotdog stuff. I notice a girl getting off the bus across the parking lot at the bus stop. I'd recognize her from a mile away: Rubee.

Rubee is wearing her Safeway shirt and she's walking fast, like maybe she's late for work. Her dark hair is loose on her shoulders.

Darius shows up and slings the grocery bags into the car, fitting them around the beer and my hockey bag.

As Rubee walks, she combs her hair back with her fingers and catches it into a thick ponytail.

Darius says, "She is so hot."

Darius is watching her too.

I say, "Hot, yes. But Rubee is beautiful."

Rubee is a senior like Darius and me, but she goes to a different school. I've never seen Rubee anywhere but here, at Safeway. We always choose Rubee's checkout line, even if hers is twice as long as the others. Rubee is worth the wait.

Darius says, "Weird that she took the bus. Her boyfriend always drops her off."

I've never seen her boyfriend, but Rubee wears a guy's ring on her thumb. Plus, a couple of months ago, she rejected Darius when he asked her out. Go figure—he asked her if she'd like to spend the night with a wild man.

I say, "You've seen Rubee's boyfriend?"

Darius nods. "He has a nice car."

I glance at my Civic. One fender is a different color and the left taillight is covered with a red plastic bag.

I say, "Maybe it's her brother."

"No." Darius turns to me. "It was her boyfriend. But she took the bus today, so that means he isn't her boyfriend anymore."

"Maybe he had to work or something."

Darius says, "From the car he drives, he makes way more money than a regular job."

"You think he sells drugs or something?" I watch as Rubee enters the Safeway. "She wouldn't go out with a guy like that."

Darius looks at me. "And you would know?"

"Yes. She's too sweet."

He says, "Sweet girls fall the hardest."

I say, "How can you be sure they broke up?"

"Let's just run with it," Darius says. "You think she's too sweet for you?"

My face grows hot. "No."

"So go ask her out."

"No."

He laughs again, and I'm getting pissed off.

I say, "Not today. I'll ask her out sometime when I'm wearing my team jacket. A hockey jacket makes a busted nose look tough." Instead of ugly. "And I'll wear my ring, my junior hockey championship ring."

Darius says, "If you don't ask her out right now, I will."

My hands curl into fists. "Like she'd go out with you, Wildman."

He shrugs. "Only one way to find out." He slams down the hatch on my car and strides toward the store.

I catch up with him. "We've got everything we need. Let's go."

But he's in the store and in Rubee's line.

Ahead of us, an old woman in sweatpants smacks coins onto the counter. She is ranting to Rubee about an expired coupon. She doesn't have much on the conveyor: bananas, toilet paper—the cheap stuff—and some liquid meal replacement old people drink. The cans of meal replacement have a red clearance sticker. They must be close to the best-before date. Maybe they've expired.

Rubee speaks quietly to the woman as she pushes several coins back to her. The woman grins, gathers the coins, grabs her bag of groceries and scuttles out of the store. The guy in front of us shovels the rest of his stuff onto the conveyor. Rubee counts the old woman's coins into the cash drawer. She looks up and sees me. She smiles.

I look at her hand. She's not wearing the ring.

I watch her scan the guy's groceries. She's wearing a black cord bracelet with a round red stone. The stone slides back and forth on her wrist as she works. But she's not wearing the ring. She smiled at me, she's not wearing the ring and we're standing in her line with nothing to buy.

I grab a pack of gum and toss it in a shopping basket.

Darius laughs. "Corbin, if you're asking her out, you'll need more time than it takes to ring in one pack of gum." He turns and snags a half-filled cart someone has left unattended. He pushes the cart into Rubee's line.

I say to him, "I'm not asking her out. I'm not ready. If she says no, I'll lose my once-in-a-lifetime chance." I peer into the cart. "Nice. You were right out of Huggies."

Behind us, a woman says, "Now where did I leave my cart?"

Darius says, "Once in a lifetime? You're asking her out, not proposing."

I pull a package out of the pile of groceries in the cart. "And animal crackers."

The woman's voice is louder now. "I swear, I left my cart right here."

Rubee looks up then, sees the woman. She glances at our cart and rolls her eyes. She picks up the security phone.

Darius says, "Oops, I seem to have someone else's cart." And he leaves it there. Just abandons the cart in the line. He walks by me and past the guy ahead of us until he's standing in front of Rubee. Rubee puts the phone down.

I elbow my way past the guy so that I'm beside Darius. I struggle to meet her eyes. "Uh, sorry about the, uh, cart."

Darius just stands there. Finally he says to me, "Anything else?"

I glance at Rubee. She looks like she's waiting for me to say something. Her eyes have little gold flecks. I feel my cheeks turn bright red. I hand her the pack of gum.

She smiles. "Just the gum? No diapers?"

I shake my head and hand her the money.

Darius sighs. He says to me, "Are you done?"

I look at my shoes.

"I'll take that as a yes." He turns to Rubee. "Riley Park, tonight. I'm saving myself for you."

She looks at him and crosses her arms. "Unlikely," she says, "on both counts."

"We'll go swimming."

"You might, but you'll freeze."

"I'm a wild man." Darius smiles at her. "I'll bring blankets."

It's not like Darius is super attractive. He's built, but he's not that tall. He spends a fortune on his hair. Maybe that's why the girls go for him. Darius reaches into a pail of plastic-wrapped flower bouquets by the check stand. He selects an arrangement of red and white roses. Water from the bouquet drips on the counter. He presents the flowers to Rubee. "These are for you," he says. "A token of my love."

Rubee takes the flowers and smiles.

Darius says, "Riley Park. Tonight. Nothing complicated, Rubee. You're your own woman. No one telling you what to do—you're in control. Come to the party if you want, bring some friends, have a few laughs, or don't. It's totally up to you."

The guy with the groceries tells us to piss off and get out of the line.

Darius ignores him. "Later, I hope," Darius says to Rubee, and he blows her a kiss.

Chapter Two

The party is just getting started, and I'm half cut when Darius decides to go cliff jumping. He peels off his shirt and jeans and stands there in his boxers. Some of the girls giggle. One of the guys from my team, Jason, high-fives Darius, but I don't see Jason or anyone else stripping down. It's October and cold. Darius is already covered in goose bumps. He looks at me. "Come on. The water will feel warm."

One of the girls circles Darius's waist with her arms, folding her hoodie around him.

I shrug, drain my beer and toss the can in a heap by the fire. "So let's do it."

The guys cheer. Riley Park is on the banks of the Riley River. On the other side of the river, across a footbridge, are sheer cliffs and then a slope up into a forest. I'm out of my clothes and jogging over the bridge before I can convince myself that we're nuts.

The cliffs are a rock wall. We climb to the highest outcrop. We've timed how long it takes a jumper to hit the water and figure that we're at least sixty feet up. That's twice the height of the highest Olympic diving platform. I'm not scared but my stomach does a slow turn, anticipating the rush. Below us, across the river, I can see our fire pit. People are looking up at us. I hear Jason shout, "The gap!"

The gap is higher still, where the rock cliffs give way to forest. We won't be able to see the water until we're in the air. We have to take a run at it in order to clear a stand of trees growing on the side of the cliff. The gap is a commitment—once we start, we can't change our minds. Otherwise we'll end up bouncing down the stone cliff or impaled on a tree.

Darius says, "We'll jump the gap together."

"Together?"

He laughs. "We've never done it before. It'll blow them away."

"Or us." We head up to the gap.

Now we're in the trees and the trail is narrow. We'll each have to run on the edge of the path. I wish I had something on my feet, although I hate swimming with shoes. Shoes are like anchors.

Darius says, "At the trees, we jump."

"No, really? I was going to run right into them."

"If we die, we die together."

"Nice thought, us dying."

"On three." And that fast, we're down the trail, over the trees and in the air.

For a moment we are weightless. We are suspended in air, motionless, and the moment extends into time. My stomach climbs into my throat. I hear the guys below, hooting, cheering. Darius and I are so close that I can touch him. Finally, we drop. The air is cold, and it whistles over my legs and chest and through my ears.

We hit water. It feels like plywood. It's cold, like the water is barely liquid. Cold closes over me, clamping my lungs so that the air inside compresses. My lungs feel like fire. I fight for the surface. We're not that far underwater, but my arms and legs feel useless. When I break the surface, Darius is already there, laughing. I suck a breath, but no air goes in. I gasp. When at last the air enters, it tears into my lungs and I cough. I spit water. Then I'm laughing too. I thrash my arms, heading for the shore.

Beside me, Darius slips into a smooth, head-up front crawl. He says, "My friend, that was a trip."

At the shore, the rocks are slimy and my fingers can't seem to bend to get a handhold. I slither out of the water on my belly. Darius is already out, shaking his wet hair on the girls, making them scream. Then I hear her voice. Rubee.

"Hey, Wildman," she says.

Rubee is looking at Darius, smiling. She's with another girl I recognize from Safeway. Darius grabs Rubee into a wet hug and she wriggles free.

Darius picks up his clothes and ducks behind a tree. I scramble to my feet and follow him. He drops his wet boxers and yanks on his jeans. Quietly, he says to me, "I knew she couldn't resist."

I pull on my pants, hating how they stick to my legs. I say, "You're an asshole, Darius."

He laughs. "You had your chance."

Suddenly I'm not cold anymore. When I speak, there's a hard edge to my voice. "You didn't give me a chance."

His grin fades. "I don't own her, Corbin. If she wants to hook up with you, she will." He shakes his head. "What's your problem, anyway?"

I hate it when he shakes his head like that. It's like he drops the gloves but won't fight. I don't try to keep my voice down—I don't care who hears. I say, "My problem, Darius?" I shove him in the chest, hard. He stumbles out from behind the tree. "My problem is that you're here."

Everyone goes quiet. Jason mutters, "Corbin's drunk and looking for a fight. What a surprise."

Rubee moves to Darius's side.

Darius says to Jason, "Leave him alone." To me, he says, "We're okay?"

I glance at Rubee. She's wearing a white sweater and jeans. I've never seen her except in her Safeway uniform. She's wearing the same red stone bracelet. Her hand goes to Darius's hip. Nope, I don't have a chance. With a sigh, I say to Darius, "Yes, we're okay." I give Jason a shove. "And I'm not drunk. Yet."

I storm over to the cooler and grab a six-pack. I pound one back and then another. I guess I drink them all—and I pass out.

When I wake up, the fire is burning high. I see Darius by the edge of the trees, taking a leak. I can't see Rubee. Where is everybody?

I drag myself to my feet. Darius looks up. I say to him, "Where's Rubee?"

"She and her friend left hours ago." Darius zips his pants. "Have a nice nap?"

I say, "Everyone is gone."

"Jason just left. We burned all the firewood in the park keeping warm." Darius puts out his hand for my car keys, and I give them to him.

Darius could have left too. He could have left with Rubee or the others. But he waited. I say, "Thanks."

He laughs. "Corbin, you are such an asshole." He throws his arm around my shoulders.

Something crashes into the back of my head. The impact sends me flying. At first I think that Darius hit me, but when I turn, I see three guys are on top of him, and one of them is swinging a steel bar.

Chapter Three

Swimming. The guys are swimming in front of my eyes, three guys. They're wearing hoods, but I can see their faces, sort of. Their faces are blurry, like I'm seeing them from underwater. The guy with the bar, he's swinging it behind him and over his head. The steel bar arcs and I see it like a blade, a cold gray blade, cutting open the night. The bar crunches against Darius's shoulder, and he pitches forward onto his knees. I hate that Darius is in the dirt. I hate that he's on his knees. I blink, trying to clear my vision, and I struggle to get up. Someone boots me under the chin. My head rockets backward and my teeth puncture my tongue.

The steel bar swings again, thudding against Darius's back. Darius makes a whooshing noise, that's all. Another guy is kicking him in the ribs. Darius reaches for the guy's foot, puts his hands on the guy's boot as it lands on him again. It looks like Darius is kissing the guy's boot. The guy with the bar swings it like an axe over Darius's head.

There is a guy between me and the one with the bar, but it doesn't matter. I launch myself at the guy with the bar, knocking him off his feet. My fist connects with his face so hard that I feel bones give way. Then the bar is in my hands, and I'm swinging it, bashing it into someone more by chance than skill, but it still doesn't matter. It just matters that one guy is hurling puke in a perfect spiral as I hit him again, taking out his knees. Blood is running into my eyes and I can't see, but I swing that bar, my hands slipping on blood and snot and puke. Somewhere I hear sirens, and then there's nothing to hit. They're running. I take off after them, the path crazy under my feet. I hear a car engine, a nice car, and gravel spewing. I drop the bar and claw at my eyes, trying to see. The car has no lights. It slews around in the lot, and then it's gone.

Darius. I reel along the path back to the fire pit. In the light of the fire, I make out his shape on the ground. I crumple beside him. "Darius." Don't move him. My head is pounding, an actual noise, like a helicopter is inside my head. "Darius!" I shout it, but I can't hear my own voice. Darius's eyes are open, but he's not looking at me. Then I feel hands on my shoulders.

They're back.

I'm on my feet and my fist is round-housing and I feel flesh. I hit again, and teeth crack under my fist. I hear voices and they're shouting and a light burns into my face. I'm blind in the light, swinging, and I plant my fist into the big square face of a cop.

The Taser hits me in the chest. I don't know it's a Taser when it hits me, but in a split second, I know.

Every muscle in my body goes stiff. My teeth bang down, my lips crank back, my neck is like wire rope. It's the worst pain, and in every muscle, every single muscle. I fall backward and I can't stop myself, can't even put my hands out to break the fall. The pain of the Taser is like my body is the puck on the end of a slap shot, and the slap shot never ends. I call out to the cops to stop. I've never felt anything hurt so badly, but I'm totally aware of the cops. It's like I'm watching them in a movie, a really scary movie, and I can't move to turn it off. They're talking to me, telling me to calm down, and I'm screaming at them to turn it off, just turn it off.

I don't think it's ever going to stop. I'm going to die. But then it does. The pain vanishes. The cop with the Taser says, "That was five seconds, big guy. Do you want another?"

Five seconds. The pain is gone, and at first all I feel is relief. I roll into a ball on the ground. I've never been more exhausted, like I've just done a week of training camp. Five seconds. Do I want another? I decide that the

Chapter Four

The cop leans over the gurney as the paramedics wheel me into the emergency room. He has his notebook out, asking me questions, and he talks funny, which I mention.

The cop gives me a look that makes me regret the comment. "That's because you loosened my teeth," he says.

"I wouldn't have hit you," I say. "It's just that I thought you were these guys."

"These guys."

"These guys. There were three of them. I don't know who they were. They just showed up, started beating on me and Darius."

Darius.

"Where is Darius?" I ask.

The cop glances at the paramedic, then back to me. "The kid on the ground?"

I nod.

"He's your friend?"

No, I just get into fights defending random strangers. "Yes, he's my friend."

The cop writes something in his notebook. "The docs are with him now." He wipes his nose and winces, like he forgot that he just got hit in the face. He says, "These guys, you don't know who they are?"

My head is pounding. "No."

"Why do you think they came after you?"

I think of Rubee. I say, "I have no idea."

The cop looks at me. "So you and Darren were just in the wrong place at the wrong time."

"Darius."

The cop looks at his notebook.

My best friend. The guy who has been my friend longer than anyone. "My friend, his name is Darius."

"Darius," the cop says. "Right. So you and Darius don't have any connection with these guys."

"Right."

"How many guys?"

"Three. I told you that."

"What were they wearing?"

I replay the scene in my head. Everything appears as gray. Gray clothes. Gray skin. Gray steel. I say, "Do you mean were they wearing colors, some kind of gang?"

He shrugs.

"I don't know. I don't think so."

My head is pounding so hard I'm surprised the cop doesn't hear it too.

The paramedics wheel me into a curtained cubicle. A nurse appears, and she's gray too, her gray hair held back in a ponytail. She snaps on new gloves and greets the cop. "Hey, Rex. Nice goal your son made last game."

Rex. The name makes me think of a bulldog. I snort.

Rex is a mind reader, apparently. He turns to me and says, "That's Officer Rex to you."

The nurse takes a chart from the end of the gurney and flips it open. She speaks to me while she reads the chart. "How much did you drink tonight?"

"My head hurts."

She moves up beside my head and peers into my eyes. She recoils, using the chart to fan the air in front of her face. "I'd say you had a fair bit."

Officer Rex says, "His head is cracked open at the back."

Without moving my head, the nurse peels up the bandage and the pounding gets louder. "Nice. Looks like he'll need surgery." She looks at me. "We're going to have to get rid of what's in your stomach."

I'm wondering what she means, when she holds up a package. Inside the package is a length of clear tube.

Officer Rex grimaces.

The nurse nods at the paramedics. One moves to each side of the gurney. The nurse opens the package and fits an end on the tube.

Then she squirts on a blob of clear gel. "If you don't fight this, it won't be so bad."

She pries open my mouth and jams the tube to the back of my throat.

My eyes fly open and I gag, but I can't clear the tube. I can't breathe. I reach for the nurse, but the paramedics clamp my arms. I gag again, and the tube slithers into me. I can feel it, actually feel it moving in my gut. I start to puke.

Officer Rex steps back from the gurney.

The nurse vacuums the spew out of my mouth. "We're in." She eyes the orange liquid coming up the tube. "Looks like hot dogs."

I puke again, and the puke tastes like tube and the gel crap, which tastes worse than puke, if that's possible.

The back of my throat is on fire.

I retch, wishing I could expel the tube, wishing I could reach in and yank it out, wishing I could get the paramedics off my arms and I'd rip that tube out and I don't care if my entire stomach comes with it.

The nurse puts her hand on my chest. "Easy."

Does she know I can't breathe?

My eyes fill and I taste snot streaming from my nose.

Get this thing.

Out.

Of.

Me.

One of the paramedics has broken into a sweat. The other is practically sitting on me. The nurse adjusts the tube. I retch again.

"That's going to feel better," she says.

For who? The tube is red hot, nuking my puke, searing my throat.

She clicks off the pump. She looks at me with warning in her eyes. "Do not move."

And the tube is out. Even the paramedics seem relieved. She hands me a paper tray and I spit the last of it. My throat feels like I just drank gasoline. I suck air until my lungs hurt.

On the other side of the curtained partition, a monitor starts to beep. I hear someone yell, "Crash cart!"

The nurse swears softly, peels off her gloves and disappears around the curtain.

Officer Rex moves next to me.

I hear the sound of running feet and a cart.

"Clear!"

Officer Rex is watching me.

Again I hear it. "Clear!"

Officer Rex speaks quietly. "He's going to be all right."

Who?

From behind the curtain, I hear, "Stay with us, Darius!"

Darius.

I look at Officer Rex. His eyes flick from the curtain to me, back to the curtain.

"I need to see my friend."

"Not now."

"No. I really need to see my friend." I wrestle one arm free of the straps.

One of the paramedics calls out, "We're going to need some help in here!"

I've got the other arm free, and I'm just about off the gurney when the nurse appears. Her hair has come loose from the ponytail and hangs damp on one side of her face. She sets a syringe against the inside of my arm.

Maybe it's in my head. Maybe it's Darius, but I hear the drone of a heart monitor flatlining.

My veins are cold steel. Officer Rex swims in front of my face. And then there is nothing.

Chapter Five

The nurse is adjusting a bag of fluid that hangs over my bed. My eyelids feel like lead. I struggle to open my eyes wide enough that I can see her. The nurse looks down at me and then glances at the clock. She moves to the end of the bed, opens a clipboard and makes a note. "Nice to see you awake, Corbin."

I blink, trying to clear my vision. It's not the nurse from the ER, the one who pumped my stomach. This nurse is small with dark hair.

"Where am I?"

She looks at me and smiles. "What did you say?"

I try to clear my throat. It feels like the sides of my throat are stuck together. I'm in the hospital. That much is clear. Around me, machines beep and blink. I can't see another bed—I must have my own room. What I want to know is where is Darius? I work a tiny wad of spit down my throat. "Water."

The nurse moves to a table by the bed. She fills a plastic cup partway with water, then puts a bending straw into the cup. She holds the straw to my lips.

It's warm, but it tastes sweet, like the best thing I've ever drank.

"Slowly," the nurse says.

As if on cue, water goes down the wrong way and I cough, spitting water across the sheet.

She says, "You've been out for a while. The surgery was more complicated than the doctors expected." The nurse puts the water back on the table. "Your parents were here. We just sent them home to rest."

I bring my hand in front of my face. I notice a tube taped on top of my hand. The tube connects to a needle piercing my vein. My fingers feel stiff and my hand itches where the needle sticks in. I lift my hand to my head.

The nurse says, "They had to open your skull. The surgeon will be in later to talk to you."

They had to open my skull? That can't be good. When I touch my head, all I feel is tape.

I say, "Did they put it all back?"

The nurse looks at me, her eyebrows furrowed. "Sorry?"

"My brain."

She still looks confused.

"Never mind. It was a joke."

The nurse checks my pulse and then bustles around the bed, straightening the sheet.

I say, "I need to go see Darius."

Her hands pause on the sheet.

I repeat, "Darius. He came to the hospital when I did. We're friends."

Her tone softens. "You're our only patient in the ICU."

The ICU. Intensive care. That's where they put you if you're really screwed. Darius was worse off than me—he'd be in intensive care too. I say, "If Darius isn't in the ICU, maybe he's in the regular U."

Again with the eyebrows.

"Could you please just check? His name is Darius…"

She sighs. "Why don't you wait until your mom and dad come back?"

"Why? What will they do that you can't do?"

The nurse puts her hand on my arm. I don't know why that bothers me so much, but I want to flick it off. She says, "Your friend." She takes a breath. "He didn't make it."

Now her dark hair is fading to gray, and I see the emergency room nurse, and I hear the heart-rate monitor from behind the curtain. Darius's heart-rate monitor. And I remember now the sound it made when his heart stopped.

I swallow. "No, you're wrong. They started his heart. Maybe he's in the heart ward or something."

The nurse pats my arm, and now I am pissed off. She says, "Corbin, your friend died."

I bat her arm so that she knocks the water cup over. I blink again and again. Now there are two dark-haired nurses, now three, swimming in front of my face. "Get out."

She picks up the cup and sets it on the table. "I'll just get some paper towel and mop that up."

I scream, and my throat feels like raw meat. "Get out!"

The nurse presses a button on the wall.

"Out!"

Another nurse throws open the door. Right behind her I see the square shape of Officer Rex. He says, "Good. You're awake." He strides up to the bed. "You need to answer some questions."

He pulls a notebook from his pocket. Something shines on his front teeth. It looks like he's wearing braces.

I say, "She said Darius is dead." I motion with my hand to the nurse.

Officer Rex nods. "That can't really surprise you."

I swipe tears from my eyes.

Officer Rex hands me a tissue. To the nurses, he says, "Leave us for a few minutes, would you?"

When the nurses are gone, he turns to me. "You were pretty mad at your friend."

"No."

"That's what people are telling me. That you and Darius had a fight."

"What people? Jason? He wants my starting spot on the team. He'd do anything to drag me down."

"Maybe you'd like to beat up Jason too."

"I would, but I didn't beat up Darius. I told you what happened. We got jumped, or Darius got jumped and I happened to be there."

"Wrong place at the wrong time." He runs his tongue over his teeth. "Seems pretty severe to just randomly beat a guy. Makes sense that there's a reason."

"It doesn't make sense. Like, how can this make sense?"

He shrugs. "It makes sense that about ten people told me you roughed up Darius earlier in the evening. It makes sense that you got drunk and passed out." He scratches his head with the pen. "Your prints are all over the weapon."

"So, what, like I cracked open my own head?"

"You fell when you got Tasered."

"Someone hit me in the back of the head."

"Did you see who hit you? Maybe Darius hit you. Maybe you gave back a little better than you got."

I am suddenly so tired. "I'm going to tell you everything, okay? I just have to know. Is Darius dead?"

He nods. "He died yesterday morning. Twice they restarted his heart. The second time, he hung on just long enough for his mom to get here."

A man in green scrubs opens the door.

Officer Rex puts the notebook back in

his pocket. He turns to me and says, "Now it's a murder charge. Better get yourself a lawyer."

Chapter Six

Officer Rex moves back from the bed. The man in green introduces himself as the surgeon. He shines a light in my eyes and then flips open the clipboard at the end of the bed.

The surgeon says to me, "You're lucky to be alive."

But Darius is dead.

He says, "Whoever did this to you, they wanted to do some real damage."

I glance over at Officer Rex. His eyes narrow.

The surgeon continues, "You received a high-energy direct blow to the skull, small surface area, with a blunt object, probably a baseball bat."

Officer Rex steps up. "Or a steel bar."

The surgeon shrugs. "Or a steel bar. Centrifugal spread of fragments from the point of maximum impact—"

Officer Rex interrupts. "What?"

The surgeon sighs. "Corbin took it straight across the back of the head, basically. The assailant was at least as tall as him. Depressed open fracture, contaminated, with ensuing hematoma—"

Again, Officer Rex breaks in. "As tall as Corbin?"

The surgeon nods. "Maybe a bit taller, but not much."

Darius is shorter. Was shorter.

The surgeon takes a breath and continues. "I can only tell you what the injury tells me. Fracture pattern, type, extent and position determine causative force. Assessment of sustained injury indicates epidural hematoma." He closes the clipboard and, finally, looks at me. "We went in and elevated the fracture. The next few weeks will tell us the extent of damage to the brain. You'll be in ICU until we assess the risk of seizure."

Brain damage? Seizure?

"No physical activity that might compromise the injury," the surgeon says. "No alcohol or drugs."

I find my voice. "I have hockey practice."

His eyebrows lift. "Uh, hockey would be a physical activity that might compromise the injury." Then, like he's sorry for making me sound like an idiot, he says, "No contact sports. No running. A brisk walk is good."

"I'm on the starting line in our next game."

"No hockey."

"I'm getting scouted."

He shrugs. "No hockey."

I say, "How long before I can play?"

The surgeon returns the clipboard to the end of the bed. "Don't push your luck." He goes to the door and pulls it open. "We saw more of your brain than we ever like to see."

He pauses, like he's considering what he's about to say. When he speaks, he sounds tired. "With this kind of trauma, it's not just the injury. If we could fix the other stuff, then we'd be doing something." He leaves and the door closes behind him.

Officer Rex clears his throat. "So your friend wasn't tall enough to do this to you, and it didn't happen when you fell. Looks like you were attacked."

"I'll cancel my call to the lawyer."

"Not yet. You'll be charged for resisting arrest at the very least. And if I get my way, you'll pay for this dental work." He bares his teeth to reveal metal bands on his top and bottom teeth. "It's a splint. Temporary, I hope. Apparently it will keep my teeth from falling out. The guys at the station say I have braces. They think it's hilarious."

I say, "It was an accident. I thought you were one of them."

He retrieves his notebook from his pocket. "One of them. Who would that be?"

"I told you, I don't know. I've never seen the guys before."

"This kind of attack isn't random," he says. "You pissed someone off in a big way. Good thing a neighbor called in a complaint that your fire was so big you were going to burn down the park. Otherwise, we wouldn't have shown up. You might be dead too."

I think back to the night. It plays in black and white. "We went cliff jumping, me and Darius."

I think about how, when we jumped, we were so close I could touch him. If I reached out my hand, I would have been able to touch his shoulder.

I hear Darius's laugh. I watch him swimming.

Red and white roses.

Officer Rex stares at me. Was I talking out loud? I say, "Then a girl came."

Officer Rex tilts his head. "A girl?"

"Rubee. I don't know her, not really. She works at Safeway, the one near Riley Park."

Officer Rex writes something in his notebook. "So what about the girl? Was she with you?"

My eyes hurt, like the light is suddenly too bright. "No. Not with me."

"With Darius?"

Wildman.

"No. I don't know. Maybe."

Probably.

I say, "She didn't stay long."

"So she wasn't there when you were attacked?"

Red and white roses, floating on the water, but they weren't on the water. There were no roses. I'm imagining them.

I say, "She wasn't there."

"Looks like you're the only witness." Officer Rex pockets his notebook. "Maybe you'll think of something you missed. If I'm going to find the guys who killed Darius, I don't have a lot to go on."

Darius. How can he be gone?

Officer Rex moves to the door and then turns to look at me. He says, "I'm sorry about your friend." He leaves.

Chapter Seven

I've been in the hospital for a few days, and already the food is old—in every way. I push aside the tray of hospital lunch—tuna sandwich made with bread that curls up at the edges, and vegetable soup with orange-colored grease blobs on the surface.

Officer Rex is here, again. He takes the sandwich. He sniffs it and says, "It's perfectly good."

"It's all yours," I say.

Maybe my parents will bring me real food, like a pizza. They come every night after work. There's a price to their visits. My mom always cries. My dad always looks like I did this to him. If I cracked my head open in a hockey game, it would be okay. It's not okay that I was drunk at a party—like it really makes any difference.

I watch Officer Rex devour the tuna sandwich in three bites. He says, "I guess you prefer hot dogs."

I shudder. I say, "Uh, you've got some sandwich stuck in your braces."

He tongues the front of his teeth. "It's a splint."

I hand him a carton of milk. "Here, you can have this too."

He eyes the milk and then says, "You should drink it."

"It's warm."

He shrugs. "Okay. No sense it going to waste."

By the look of his gut, Rex doesn't let much go to waste.

He swigs the milk and then swishes it in his mouth to dislodge the food bits from his dental work. If I was hungry before, I'm sure not hungry now. He finishes the milk and wipes his mouth on the back of his hand.

He says, "I brought some pictures for you to look at—see if you recognize any of the guys that attacked you."

He hands me a sheet of about fifty small photos. I say, "What are these, mug shots?"

"Driver's license photos." He burps. "We only have mug shots if a guy's been arrested for something."

I push the button that turns on the light over the bed. "The pictures are so small I can hardly see them."

"Take your time."

The photos are all of young men with similar features. I scan the photos and point to one. "This could be the guy with the bar." I move my finger down the sheet. "Or this guy." I hand him back the sheet. "There are about ten pictures that look like the same guy."

"Did the guy with the bar have any distinguishing marks—a tattoo, maybe, or a scar?"

"It was dark. They hit us from behind." I think about Darius on the ground. "I didn't get a good look at any of them."

Officer Rex sighs. "Try again." He hands me the sheet.

I hold the sheet up closer to my eyes. Now the images blur. My head hurts from looking so hard. I say, "There's a good reason I'm looking at these?"

"Maybe. I watched the girl, Rubee, and I happen to know her boyfriend. It's her boyfriend, right?"

He says it like I should know. I say, "Rubee doesn't have a boyfriend."

"Oh?"

"She used to. But she dumped him."

"To go to Riley Park with you guys?"

"No. Or maybe he dumped her. I don't know. All I know is that she doesn't have a boyfriend."

He nods. "Well, it looks like they're back together."

I study the page of photographs. I point to one. "Is it this guy?"

"Don't guess."

I point to another. "No, it's this guy."

He looks at the photo. "Are you sure?"

My stomach knots. "No one looks like their driver's license photo. How can I be sure?"

"Because it's all we've got."

I say, "I thought you said you knew this guy. So he's a criminal, right?"

"No," he says. "He's been a person of interest in several crimes. But we haven't nailed him yet."

I throw the sheet of photos at him. "So you know who he is and you're making me tell you?"

He says, "I don't know anything. I wasn't there."

"But you think Rubee's boyfriend, or whoever he is, came after us."

"You tell me."

"What does Rubee say?"

He rubs his temples. "Not much."

"But you talked to her?"

"I did." He pauses, like he's choosing his words. "I suggested she see a doctor about her eye."

White-hot adrenaline squirts into my spine.

He continues, "She said she walked into a door."

"It wasn't a door." My head starts to pound. "And it wasn't Darius."

He nods. "I'm pretty sure you're right about that."

I say, "So the bastard kills my best friend and beats up a girl and you let him walk free?"

He sighs. "We don't have anything to charge him with."

"Give me the photos."

He puts the sheet of photos on the table by the bed. "I'll leave them with you. Maybe you'll remember something."

No pressure. Not like it all depends on me.

I say, "When you talked to Rubee, did she know?"

"About Darius?" He lifts one shoulder. "Hard to say. She seems scared."

I want to ask him if my name came up. Did she ask about me? Does she care if I'm okay? I say, "Do you think she had anything to do with it?"

He tilts his head. "I wondered. What do you think?"

I think of roses, of the red stone bracelet she wears. "No way. She's not like that."

Then I think of the black cord tether on her wrist. Did the boyfriend give her that bracelet? I think of Darius asking her if she'd ever spent the night with a wild man. "I mean, why? Why would she be that mad?"

Officer Rex watches me, like he's waiting for me to answer my own question.

Darius would never hit her. I wouldn't.

I was so drunk.

I say, "I don't know anything anymore."

"That much is clear." Officer Rex tosses the photos onto my chest. "Let's hope you start remembering something."

Chapter Eight

The physiotherapist stands at the side of the treadmill. He's hooked me up to a machine to measure my heart rate. "Start out walking slowly," he says. "If you feel like it, you can pick up the pace."

The clinic is in the basement of the hospital. I've been coming down every afternoon. The first time, I had to take a wheelchair. Today I took the stairs. Just getting out of bed is tiring, but I'll do anything if it gets me out of the hospital.

I look down at my runners. One shoelace is undone. I bend to do it up.

"You okay?" the physiotherapist says.

My fingers feel like I have gloves on. I can't seem to get the shoe done up.

"I'm fine."

"It's normal," he says. "Sometimes patients with brain injuries have to relearn a few things."

Like tying shoes? I don't think so. I manage a loose knot. The ends of the shoelaces hang onto the treadmill. I stand up and say, "Let's go."

The physiotherapist checks his stopwatch. "When you're ready."

I take a step and the treadmill resists. Another step, and finally the mat begins to move. I feel my face already turning red. I concentrate on putting one foot in front of the other.

"Good work," he says. "That's sixty seconds."

I groan.

The physiotherapist grins. "Have you ever jumped the gap at Riley Park?"

He makes conversation, but we have nothing to talk about. The first time I came to the clinic, I told him what happened, how I got beat up at Riley Park. Now it's like he's my buddy.

He continues, "I used to jump the gap. One year I did it in November. I actually broke through ice."

"Uh-huh." Even if I wanted to talk, I'd find it difficult. I'm busy breathing.

He says, "It was just a patch of ice, more like thin glass. But the water was so cold that I thought I was going to freeze to death."

"Jumped lately?" I manage to ask between breaths.

He shakes his head. "Nope. At some point I figured out that the risk outweighed any possible fun."

"You got old."

He shrugs. "If thirty is old, it's not a bad thing, considering the alternative."

The alternative. I didn't tell the physiotherapist about Darius. He wants me to walk on a treadmill, and I can do that. On a treadmill, it doesn't make a difference that my best friend is dead. In everything else, it makes a difference. It makes a difference that when I brush my teeth I use the same kind of toothpaste that Darius used. I don't eat green peas, ever, after Darius puked green peas in seventh-grade science class. When I listen to music, I hear songs Darius downloaded. That stuff makes a difference.

Yesterday, I called Darius's cell phone. I just wanted to hear his voice on the recording.

The physiotherapist clicks his stopwatch. "Okay. Take a break."

I grab the rails alongside the treadmill and step off. "Toss me my water, would you?"

He hands me my water bottle. It's my hockey team's bottle, made of stainless steel, with the team logo on the side. My teammates signed their names on the bottle, writing stupid things like "At least it was just your head." Jason brought it for me.

Jason couldn't be too sad about me being in the hospital. Now he's got a shot at playing.

I open the lid on the water bottle and drink.

The physiotherapist says, "Water bottles will kill us. If the plastic ones don't give us cancer, that kind"—he points to my water bottle—"will give us Alzheimer's."

I know what he's talking about—the metal that's in pots and antiperspirant. What is it called? I say, "My bottle is stainless steel."

The other kind of metal, it's the same stuff as tinfoil. House siding too. What is it?

He says, "My mother made my porridge every day in an aluminum pot. I'll be lucky if I don't lose my marbles."

Aluminum. That's it.

I say, "Can people get their memory back?"

"Not people with Alzheimer's. Something happens in the brain. It changes."

"What about other people?"

He looks at me. "Are you having trouble with your memory?"

"No." I snap the lid back on the water bottle. "Shouldn't we get back to work?"

"This time we'll do it with special effects." He turns to the heart-rate monitor and flips a switch. The sound of my heart reverberates from the machine. "Sound and lights."

I step on the treadmill and start to walk. At first, the sound of my heart stays the same. I try to keep my breathing slow and calm. It's just a walk. I could walk all day like this. I feel my face getting warm. The sound of my heart increases in tempo.

Some memories I wish I would lose. Like Rubee's voice, how she called Darius "Wildman." I remember Darius and Rubee at the fire, or I think I do. It must have been before I passed out. Rubee was standing close to Darius, and he had his arm around her. I remember how her dark hair shone, like it caught the light from the fire. I remember how she threaded her fingers through Darius's belt loop.

"Take it easy, Corbin."

My heart rate is thudding, the sound keeping pace with the thud in my head.

Officer Rex thinks I know more than I'm saying. But I don't know anything.

I don't know if what I remember is real.

I remember the sound of Darius's heart monitor. I remember the sound it made when his heart stopped.

"Corbin?"

I stumble and the treadmill pulls my feet out from under me.

"The rails!"

I grab the rails. The physiotherapist snaps off the monitor. He says, "You just about lost it."

"I'm not getting any better." I'm breathing so hard I can barely speak. "When am I going to get better?"

He says, "Well, you've lost some muscle tone and your coordination is still impaired."

"When?"

"It could be that your perception has been affected, how you judge where you are. I could run some tests…"

"Just tell me. When will I be normal?"

He waits a long time before he answers. "This kind of injury, Corbin, redefines what is normal. I'm not saying you won't see some improvement. But you can't expect everything back the way it was."

Nothing is the way it was. That's just the way it is. Welcome to my new normal.

"We're done," I say. I pick up my water bottle. "Here's a souvenir." I lob it to him and he catches it. "Stainless steel, guaranteed not to make you crazy."

My shoelace has come undone again, but I'm not going to try tying it again, not now. I just have to get out of here.

Chapter Nine

The air feels cold, like the season changed from fall to winter in the weeks I was in hospital. It's raining. I crank the heater in my car, waiting for my breath to clear from the windshield. If anyone knew I was in my car, they'd have something to say about it. I'm supposed to be home in bed. But anyone normal is either at work or at school, so no one has to know. I rev the engine. A spot the size of a grapefruit clears on the windshield. If I hunch over the steering wheel, I can see out of the clear space. I put the car into gear and head out.

I recognize other cars in the Riley Park lot. Jason's car is here. He must have skipped last class. I pull my hat lower on my head to cover the bald space from the surgery.

The trail into the park feels long. People walking their dogs greet me as they pass. Sometimes a dog runs up to me, but I don't stop to pat it. I watch each step on the uneven path.

When I near the fire pit, I hear voices. People are crying. Then I see Jason and a group of others. Plastic-wrapped flowers lie heaped on the ground. On top of the pile is a brown teddy bear. It's not Darius's funeral—I missed that when I was in the hospital. But it feels like a funeral. I stop on the path, suddenly unsure if I should intrude.

One of the girls sees me and runs over to me. She's been crying—mascara runs down her cheeks. She pulls me over to the others.

Jason is standing with his hands in his pockets. He gives me a long look. "You're out."

"Nice to see you too."

Jason says, "I could have picked you up. We skipped last class, just wanted to come out here. You know, to remember Darius."

The way he says it, I know what he's thinking: Too bad it was Darius. Too bad it wasn't me. I say, "Yeah, I do know. Too bad Darius is dead. Too bad no one stuck around that night."

Jason looks like he'd like to say something, but he doesn't.

I continue, "Not that you'd have been any use in the fight."

Jason pulls his hands out of his pockets. "From what I heard, you guys didn't have a chance."

"From what I heard," I say, "you thought I did it."

More girls are crying.

Rain is falling hard now. Rain bounces off the teddy bear's head.

Darius didn't even like teddy bears.

I nudge the bear with the toe of my shoe. It tumbles off the pile.

Jason moves between me and the pile of flowers. He says, "No one thinks you killed Darius."

Rain is running down his face. He could be crying.

A girl retrieves the bear and brushes mud from it. She holds the bear like a doll.

Rain gathers in puddles. A loose flower tumbles into a puddle. It's a rose, a red rose, and it floats on the puddle.

It makes me mad to see the rose. It shouldn't be here. None of this should be here. I turn to Jason. "I fought for him. I'm missing a piece of my brain because I stayed and fought."

Jason's shoulders tense. He says, "If Darius had left with the rest of us, maybe there wouldn't have been a fight."

I throw a punch and my fist glances against Jason's cheek. It hardly registers on him, but it sets me off balance and I fall back into the mud.

All the girls are crying now.

Jason isn't hurt. I'm too weak to hurt him. He offers his hand to help me up but I knock it away. I say, "I fought three guys. I fought them until they ran away."

Jason sighs. "Or they ran when they heard the police sirens."

I struggle to my feet. "You weren't there. How do you know anything?"

He doesn't know anything. Does he? Could Jason look at the photos and see the guy's face? I say to him, "Were you there?" I hate how it sounds like I'm pleading.

He shakes his head. "No, Corbin, I wasn't there. I'm sorry."

Yeah, I'm sorry too. I turn from the group and leave.

Chapter Ten

At Safeway, there are no carts left. It's so busy it must be double-Airmiles day or something. But I don't need a cart—I'm not shopping.

I go to Rubee's checkout line. She's not there. I head to express because sometimes she works there. But she's not in the express line. So I go from line to line, checking each one for Rubee. She's not there.

Maybe she hasn't started her shift. I go to the coffee counter and order a coffee.

The girl behind the counter says, "Would you like that to go?"

I turn to see some empty seats at the tables. "No, I'll have it here. So not in a paper cup. A regular cup. You know."

"A mug?" She smiles.

A mug. I try to smile back. "Yes, a mug. That's what I meant."

She smiles at me as she makes it. I pay, but when I go to pick up the mug, my hand shakes so badly that I have to set it down. I slop coffee on the counter.

"Sorry," I say.

The girl grabs a cloth and wipes up the spill. "It happens to me all the time."

It doesn't happen to me. Or it didn't use to happen.

A line has formed behind me. The girl says, "Why don't I put that in a paper cup? That way you can use a lid."

That way I can get it to the table without pouring it on anyone. I say, "Sure."

She pours the coffee into a paper cup and tops it up. "Careful," she says. "It's hot."

The cup has a printed warning too, *hot, hot, hot*. Like I wouldn't know coffee is hot. But when I pick up the cup, it feels too hot to hold and I set it back down. I say to the girl, "I need to talk to Rubee."

She looks puzzled.

I say, "You know Rubee? She works here, on cash. Slim, with long dark hair? She always wears a bracelet with a red stone."

The girl nods. "Sure, I know Rubee." She studies my face, my crooked nose. "Weren't you at Riley Park?"

I remember now. She came to the party with Rubee. I say, "No, that was…" I hesitate. "That was someone else."

She says, "I heard some hockey player started the fight."

I am tired, so tired. I lean on the counter. "I need to talk to Rubee."

The girl says, "Rubee doesn't work here anymore. She's not answering her phone and she's totally off-line. It's like she's disappeared." The girl glances at the lineup of customers waiting behind me. She says, "Can I get you anything else?"

I can't trust my hands not to shake. I leave the coffee on the counter.

Outside, I have to think for a minute about where I left my car. When I find it, someone has parked so close that I can't open the driver's side door. I have to climb in over the passenger seat—Darius's seat. I bang the top of my head on the roof of the car and my hat falls off. I scramble for my hat. When I finally get behind the wheel, I'm in a sweat. I throw the car into reverse and tromp the gas. But the wheels are cranked and I rip into the side of the car next to me. At the sound of metal crunching, several people in the parking lot turn to look. I don't care. I give the car more gas and scrape out of the stall. I flip the bird at the onlookers and peel out of the lot.

Chapter Eleven

In the garage at home, I pull my hockey bag out of the back of my car and unzip it. The smell is strong, familiar. It triggers a memory of locker rooms and the way it feels to suit up before a game. Sweat smells different before a game. It stinks of fear. I used to shower right before games and I would still stink. That's how my gear smells.

I pull my jersey over my head. I feel stronger. My jersey, my pads, my helmet—

they're like armor. In my hockey gear, I feel like a warrior, like I'm someone else.

I grab a bucket from the side of the garage and turn it upside down as a seat. I kick off my runners and put on my skates.

The floor in the garage is gritty with dirt, and I try to keep my skate blades from touching the floor. The dirt will dull the blades. I bend over my skates and tighten the laces. I pull clean shoelace out of the eyelets.

My legs aren't as big around as they were. My arms, too, are smaller than before. I'm not working out—I'm losing muscle.

My coach says not to worry about hockey, that I should focus on getting better. After the first couple of games that I missed, the coach brought me game tapes and sat and watched them with me. He tried to explain the new plays, but I couldn't understand them. He doesn't come anymore.

I hear a car pull up outside the garage. I stand and open the garage door. Officer Rex gets out of his cop car.

He points to my skates. "You'll dull your blades."

I shrug. "Not like I'm skating any time soon."

He leans on the side of my car. He runs his hand along the crumpled metal. "Doing a little modification, are you?"

"I ran into a pole."

"Oh yeah." He looks at me. "At Safeway."

He knows. One of the onlookers must have got my plate. I say, "So what? The moron parked too close."

"Maybe. He got in without hitting you."

"How do you know? Maybe he hit me." I gesture to the damaged door panels on my car. "Maybe he did all this."

"I looked at his car. I talked to people. You hit him."

"This seems pretty small, you chasing a little fender bender. Don't you have a murder investigation?"

He nods. "So you were at Safeway. Looking for Rubee?"

"She doesn't work there anymore."

"I could have saved you the trip."

"I didn't start the fight. It happened like I told you. They jumped us from the back."

"The boyfriend is gone. Some family emergency."

My head is starting to pound. "What about the other two?"

"We don't have positive identification of any of them, Corbin. For what it's worth, his buddies say that if there was a fight, they weren't there. But if they were there, they were only defending themselves. No one says anything about steel bars. If you believe them, it was just a few punches."

"Obviously I don't believe them."

"I talked to a few other people, like your hockey coach." He pauses. "And the school."

I groan. "I've been in a few fights. Who hasn't?"

"Like with Jason?"

"Did he call that a fight? I barely touched him."

Officer Rex sighs. "It's bad what happened to you and Darius. But if you're fighting yourself, you're fighting the wrong guy."

"What, now you're a shrink?"

He ignores me. "I want you to leave Rubee alone."

"Why should I? It was her boyfriend. She must have told him where we were."

"He might have followed her."

"Whatever. She knows he did it. Why isn't she saying anything?"

He looks at his shoes. "I mean it, Corbin. Leave her alone."

"You're protecting her, just like you're protecting that bastard boyfriend. What about Darius? Who's on his side? What about me?"

"This might be a new concept for you, Corbin, but this is not about you. It's about getting to the truth. Sometimes it's not a straight path to the truth. Sometimes we get it right and the courts let him walk. Sometimes we don't have enough to make a charge and the guy walks. Sometimes everyone knows the guy is guilty as hell and he still walks because someone did something stupid."

A tow truck rumbles up to the curb.

Officer Rex says, "I'm impounding your car."

"Because I scratched a car in a parking lot?"

"And your license is suspended until further notice."

Blood pounds into my temples. Before I can speak, he says, "You're not safe to drive, Corbin. If you don't hit another car, you'll drive yourself off the road."

I kick my skate blade into the side of my car. "I guess I'm under house arrest."

"Stop fighting this, Corbin."

"Did you impound his car? Rubee's boyfriend's car?" An image returns to me of the parking lot at Riley Park. It's nighttime. A car slews around in the gravel. Darius said the boyfriend drove a nice car. I say to Officer Rex, "What does he drive?"

Officer Rex says, "Maybe you can tell me."

I struggle to bring the memory into focus. "Dual exhaust. A sedan."

His eyes light up. "What color?"

"Gray." No, that's just the color of the memory. "I don't know. Something light. It's new, maybe an Acura."

He pulls out his notebook. "Where did you see it?"

"In the parking lot. That night."

"What about a plate? Did you get a plate number?"

In my memory I can't even see the plate. I'm not sure I even saw the car. "No."

He says, "You didn't see a plate? What about one number? Did you see even one number?"

"No!"

"That's okay," he says. "Maybe your memory will come back."

Sometimes memory doesn't come back.

"You're doing great. But, Corbin," he says, "you've got your pads on top of your jersey."

I look down. Sure enough, I've put stuff on in the wrong order.

He walks out to meet the tow-truck driver.

Chapter Twelve

Just one number. I sit with my math book open in front of me. Numbers float on the page. One number? I can't remember even one number from that license plate. I strain to focus on the math problem. The numbers swim. With a sigh, I snap the book closed.

The house is quiet. The clock over the stove ticks, marking seconds. Then the minute hand clicks. Seconds to minutes. Minutes to hours. How many hours until my dad gets home? How many more hours watching him watching me. Are you working out, Corbin? Are you trying? If you try, you can play again. Then my life is worth living again.

How many hours in a lifetime? How many in Darius's lifetime?

I pick up the phone. I don't have to remember the numbers—my fingers find them. I punch Darius's cell number.

His mother answers.

"Corbin?"

She sounds old.

My stomach turns upside down. "I'm sorry. I didn't think his phone would be on. The other times I called, it wasn't on."

I can hear her breathing. She says, "Corbin, you know, don't you? You know that Darius is gone."

Gone. He's dead. I say, "Yes, of course I know. I'm sorry."

"You were close. This must be hard for you."

This throws me. Like, how could she say this about me when she must be dying inside?

I say, "Are you doing okay?" She just buried her son. How could she be okay? I say, "I mean, if there's anything I can do…"

I hear her take a breath. "Sometimes I turn on his phone so I can hear his message."

"I know. I just want to hear his voice."

She says, "I can see who he talked to, right? And his text messages. It's like a record. It's like I can live a little more with him." She starts to cry.

I say, "I'm sorry. I won't call again."

"No," she says, "it's all right. You're not the only one who calls. Sometimes people haven't heard and I have to tell them, but other times it's his friends. Girls, mostly. We're all just looking for some way to have him back."

I say, "There's a girl, Rubee. Does she call?"

"Rubee? I don't think so."

"Did she call him the night he…" I don't want to use the word "died." I say, "…the night it happened?"

"No. Officer Rex asked me the same thing." She excuses herself and I hear the sound of her blowing her nose. She continues, "You have to stay strong, Corbin. For Darius. You can't lose yourself too."

"I'm not."

She says, "We want him back, but we can't have him back. One of these days I'll wake up and I'll know that he's gone, but right now I open my eyes and I'm happy for a second—until I remember."

"I'm sorry." How many times can I tell her I'm sorry?

She says, "Come and see me sometime if you want. See your friends. Just live, Corbin." She hangs up.

Chapter Thirteen

Snow falls in the afternoon, slanted on the wind. My bike tires crunch in the snow as I pedal to Riley Park. I have to get off and walk around the corners because the tires have no traction in the snow. I didn't bother to find gloves, and my hands are cold. Snow soaks through my runners.

At Riley Park, the parking lot is criss-crossed with tire tracks. There are a few cars in the lot, dog walkers maybe, but I don't see anyone around. I drop my bike by the side of the path and walk into the park.

At the fire pit, the pile of flowers is covered with fresh snow. I can make out the shape of the teddy bear. I get why people leave the flowers. But I'd leave them where Darius was most alive. I think back to the night when Darius and I jumped from the cliffs. That's where he's most alive, in that moment, suspended in time. Beside the pile, not covered in snow, I see a bundle of red and white roses. I pick up the roses.

On the frozen river, the wind riffs new snow across the blue-white skin of ice. Around me, the cliffs are somber, like they're waiting. I gaze up at the gap, imagining how it looked when Darius and I appeared out of the trees, our legs windmilling to clear the trees, so close to each other that we could touch. That's where I need to leave the flowers—right where we plunged into the river. That was the moment before everything changed. That was when the river was just ours. I head out onto the ice.

Here, in the open, the wind stings my eyes. Snow prickles against my face and my bare hands. My feet are wet. Wind whistles in my ears.

I stand and let the wind fill me. I imagine it brings the sound of Darius's voice, his laugh. The wind rings my head and my hair stands on end. In the wind, my eyes water and I let the tears stream, imagining the water that night we jumped—the night that everything changed.

I hear my name, and then I laugh because I've imagined Darius, calling me. I know he can't, but if he could call me, it would be here, at Riley Park, under the cliffs that we jumped. I loosen the roses from their wrapping.

This is where we jumped. We hit the water right here. I look down and see the water under the ice. Maybe the river froze that night, and if we could, we'd find our shapes still there, in the ice.

Again the wind howls my name. I fling the roses into the wind.

Water surges to my ankles, so cold I gasp. I look down to see roses floating on the water. The ice gives way under my feet.

Chapter Fourteen

For a second I scramble, trying to find ice instead of water, running on a backward treadmill as the ice slithers away. First I slip to my waist, and I can still feel ice with my hands. I dig my fingers against the hard surface, willing the ice to hold. But it doesn't. I hear it groan, then crack. There's nothing to grab but water, cold water, so cold that it hurts. The weight of my clothing pulls me down. Water crawls over my head. The river consumes me.

I have no breath. My lungs shrink and stick to themselves, useless. The cold is like metal. I feel metal in my blood, threading up the back of my neck into my skull. It feels like the cold could lift my skull. I close my eyes against the pain.

My runners are weights on my feet. My jeans are like steel plates. My coat flaps like steel wings, and everything, my runners, my jeans, my coat, everything drags me down. With a furious kick, I stop my downward plunge. With another kick, I feel air again on the top of my head. I throw my head back, clearing my nose and mouth in time to pull one breath into my lungs, and then I'm under the water again.

With the other foot, I peel one runner off my heel and shake my foot free. I feel the toe of my sock wafting loose. I manage to pry off the other runner. I kick, hard. Again, I'm able to breathe. Wind blows the water over my head.

I fumble with my coat zipper. My fingers are stiff, already frozen, but I get the zipper partway down. I shrug the coat off my shoulders, and for a second I'm trapped in the sleeves. The oxygen is long gone from my lungs. Frantic, I rip one arm out of the coat sleeve, then the other, and claw for the surface.

I take two breaths. I scream. One more breath and roses swirl around my head. I grab for the ice but it breaks under my arms. My coat is still around my waist, like a weight belt. As I struggle to pull myself onto the ice, my legs and body pull me under it. Under my hands, the ice breaks away in shattered panes. Shards jab me in the face. My teeth chatter so hard that I am afraid I will bite my tongue. The wind freezes my hair into spikes. Then water closes over my head and flattens my hair to my skull. My eyelashes are ice, then water, then ice.

Underwater, my heart beats in my ears. I open my mouth to scream, and cold water fills me. I gain the surface again and cough, wanting only to breathe.

I need to break the ice until it won't break under my weight. Then, maybe, I can climb out. But the ice keeps breaking. I'm getting too weak. My arms and legs grow rigid in the cold. I'm tired, so tired.

I hear my name. Water pours into my ears. My teeth stop chattering. It's quiet. I tip my head back. Around me, roses turn. I slip under the water.

Chapter Fifteen

In the ring of roses above me, I see her face. Rubee. Her hands reach down into the water. I see the red stone at her wrist, back and forth, floating across her wrist. If I reach up, I could grab her hands. I could pull her down under the water and she would die here too.

But I won't. Anger leeches out of me and I'm empty.

I see her mouth my name. She's calling me.

I'm not cold anymore. I feel warm, as if the water is the same temperature as my body.

Rubee's dark hair floats on the water with the roses. Her hands flash like fish. I feel her fingers on my head, and then they are gone.

If I kicked, if I tried, maybe I could breathe just once more.

My legs are powerless against the weight of water. But I try. I imagine I am water and that my legs are water too.

Do I hear her? Is she screaming my name?

Rubee's face is water. Behind her, the sky is white. Around her face, her hair is dark waves in the water.

Kick.

Her face vanishes and reappears.

Kick.

I feel her fingers on the back of my collar.

Kick. Help her.

She's gone. My eyes are open. I feel water in my eyes. But it's black. I blink, trying to see, but I can't see. My air is gone. My blood is water.

I close my eyes.

Something warm covers my mouth. I wait for water. But it's not water. It is air, warm air, rolling into my lungs. I'm underwater, but I'm breathing air.

My eyes fly open. I can see in shades of gray. Rubee's fingers close my lips and she retreats, her hair flowing away. It was Rubee—her air is in my lungs. I feel the strength of the air, and it begins to fade. I need more. I hold Rubee's breath, willing my cells to wring from it every bit of oxygen.

Rubee appears again. She covers my mouth with hers. Her lips are closed. I'm hungry for her air, but she won't open her mouth. I reach my hands to her face, and if I could move my fingers, I would lace my fingers in her hair.

Breathe for me, please. I cry the words, and air bubbles pour from my mouth and nose.

Then I feel her fingers pinch my nostrils. She opens her mouth over mine, and now I understand. She had to wait for me to breathe out.

She exhales, and her breath fills me. My vision clears. Again she retreats, and I think she won't appear again. I hold her breath in my lungs, imagine her breath weaving into my body, becoming mine.

Above me, I see another face, a man. He drops a loop of webbing around my chest. I feel it tighten, and I'm being lifted. I feel hands on my shoulders. My face breaks free of the water. I suck a breath, and another. I hear dogs barking. My back scrapes over the edge of the ice. I hear voices. "Pull!" I'm sliding on the ice. It's a dog leash around my chest, a purple dog leash.

Rubee huddles on the shore. Someone wraps a blanket around her. Cold pours into me and suddenly I'm shivering. My bones clatter. People strip off my clothes. They cram my arms into a dry jacket still warm from its owner. Someone covers my head with a hat.

Rubee kneels by my side. Her wet hair freezes in dark icicles. Around her face, fine hair frosts white. She's wearing someone else's jacket too. She wraps her blanket around my legs.

I say, "You brought him roses." I can hardly speak for shivering. "I saw roses here before—you brought them too."

She says, "Every day, I brought roses."

"For Darius," I say.

She nods. "Yes."

Chapter Sixteen

The man who pulled me out of the ice won't let Rubee drive. He says that I have hypothermia and I'm lucky to be alive, like I haven't heard that before. I'm beginning to believe it. Rubee and I are sitting in his van with the heater going full blast, waiting for the ambulance. He's outside with his dogs. I'm still shivering. It seems like a long time that Rubee sits without saying anything, just looking at her hands in her lap. Then she says, "I had no idea he would go after Darius."

"Your boyfriend." I'm shivering, so it's hard to talk.

"My ex-boyfriend, Quinton," she says. "I knew Quinton was jealous—he wouldn't let me go anywhere by myself—but he was the one who broke up with me. He didn't want to go out with me, but I guess he didn't want anyone else to either."

I say, "You were here? You saw what happened?"

"No. He must have followed me when I came here after work. He must have seen me with Darius. I think he came back later and waited for you guys." She pauses. "Corbin, I'm so sorry."

"I thought you might have been here."

"I wasn't. He was parked outside my house when I got home. He said he was sorry, that he was an idiot for breaking up with me."

"And you took him back?"

"I agreed to go out with him the next day, and I did. We went for ice cream. Ice cream! I hadn't heard about Darius. We sat eating ice cream, and Darius was dead." She wraps her arms around herself. She says, "I knew Quinton was in a fight—his face was pretty messed up. He's been in fights before, never when I'm around. When we were going out, he'd drop me off and then go out and party or do whatever he did. Anyway, I didn't give it too much thought. But then I went to work and I heard there was a fight at Riley Park—that Darius had been killed. I didn't believe it, but then it was on the news. So I asked Quinton if that's where he got in the fight." She lowers her eyes. "I still couldn't believe he had anything to do with it. He was always so nice to me. But he got mad."

"And then you knew."

"He told me that no one would believe me. He said that I wasn't there and how could I know anything." She starts to cry. "He said if I talked to the police, he'd make me pay."

I touch her cheekbone. Under her eye, I see a red line where her skin has split open.

She says, "Now I think back on things that happened when we were going out, stuff I just ignored because it didn't have anything to do with me. I just didn't know who he was."

I say, "It's not your fault."

"I feel so bad," she says. "Every day I come here, put my flowers on that pile and remember Darius. I didn't know him long, but he was so full of life."

I nod. He made me feel alive.

She says, "I saw you head out on the ice. People were walking their dogs and they saw you too. The man who pulled you out, he told me that it was too soon to be on the ice, that where the water flows, the ice is still thin. So I called you. You didn't hear me."

"I did hear you," I say. "I thought I was imagining it."

"Then you broke through the ice. I crawled out on the ice on my belly so I wouldn't break through. The man too. He hung on to my ankles so that I could reach you. But I couldn't lift you."

I say, "But you could breathe for me."

She says, "I saw you drowning, and it was like Quinton was holding you under the water, and me too. That's when I knew it had to stop. I couldn't be afraid anymore."

Chapter Seventeen

I stand at the boards, watching the team of six-year-olds do their best to skate from one side of the ice to the other. Officer Rex's kid, Ben, can actually skate. Ben is a nice kid. If he knows he's the star, he doesn't show it. I play all the kids the same. All of them think they're going to the NHL.

Who doesn't?

I skate a loop around the team. Coaching this level is a bit like crowd control. One of the players face-plants and slides on his belly, laughing. I lift another player out of his way.

"Okay, guys," I call, "that's it for practice. See you Sunday for the game."

I skate over and open the gate. The players tumble off the ice.

Jason waits on the other side of the boards for the kids to clear the gate. He's in his skates, no pads. He says to me, "I heard you were coaching."

"I'm not playing much hockey these days," I say. "And coaching counts for community service." That was my sentence for resisting arrest.

Jason nods. "The kids look like they're having fun."

I say, "You're here early. Your team isn't booked on the ice for another two hours."

He says, "It's your team too."

I rub the back of my head. "Maybe you didn't hear. I lost my spot in the lineup."

"I heard you were on the injured list."

"Same thing," I say.

The last kid clears the gate, and Jason steps out onto the ice. He says to me, "Let's skate some laps."

He doesn't give me a chance to say no. He skates away and I follow. I have to skate hard to keep up. I say, "I used to be faster."

He finishes my thought. "You used to be faster than me. You had a better shot too."

"I hate not playing."

For a time, he's quiet. Then he says, "It's not right, what happened to you."

I think about Darius's mom answering his cell phone. I think about the pile of flowers at Riley Park that keeps growing, and the girls at school who still cry.

I say, "It's not right, what happened to Darius."

"Manslaughter and aggravated assault." Jason shakes his head. "The guy should be going to jail for murder."

I think about Rubee, and how she and her family moved away. She said they needed some distance from the boyfriend, from everything. Rubee's testimony placed Quinton at the scene. The prosecutor couldn't prove Quinton intended to kill Darius, but Rubee's testimony was enough to get the manslaughter conviction. I have to go to court one more time for the sentencing, to give a victim impact statement.

I say, "At least Quinton won't walk."

"We can hope he gets the maximum sentence," Jason says. "What about the other two guys?"

"Officer Rex says he's working on them. Apparently I tried to kill them and they were just defending themselves."

Jason laughs. "You probably did almost kill them."

"I used to be good at fighting." I think about that day at Riley Park when I took a swing at Jason. I say, "I used to be good at fighting you."

He says, "Fight me for your spot."

My shirt is stuck to my back with sweat. I say, "Nice thought. You know I'm not coming back. I'll be lucky if I play hockey with old men."

Jason looks at me. "So don't fight me, then."

I motion for him to stop skating. I lean over with my hands on my thighs and try to catch my breath. I say, "Fine. I'll stop fighting you. Maybe now you can stop pissing me off."

He says, "I don't really think you're an asshole."

I say, "I still think you are."

He play-punches me in the arm, and it actually hurts.

He says, "I liked Darius."

Darius was everyone's friend, but he was all I had.

I say, "Everyone liked Darius."

He nods and smiles. "We had some good times."

I say, "I miss him."

I wait for Jason to say how he misses him too. But he says, "You and Darius." He shakes his head. "I can't imagine how this is for you."

Chapter Eighteen

The courtroom is packed. Officer Rex stands with me at the microphone, holding a piece of lined paper. It is my victim impact statement. I wrote it out and asked Officer Rex to read it for me. Jason and kids from school stand along the back wall. I wipe my hands on my pants. Quinton sits at a table with his lawyer, waiting for his sentence. He won't make eye contact with me. Officer Rex studies the paper. He starts to read but stumbles on the words. He says, "I'm sorry. I can't read it."

He can read it. He just can't understand what I wrote. My face feels hot.

Officer Rex hands the paper to the judge. The judge looks at it. Her eyebrows lift, and she hands the paper back to me. She says, "Corbin, can you tell us what this paper says?"

From the back of the courtroom, Jason gives me a thumbs-up.

I say to her, "Sometimes I can't remember words. I know what I want to say, but I can't seem to put the right words on the paper." I clear my throat and try to read. But I give up and let the paper drop to the floor.

I say, "I don't know who I am anymore."

I take a breath.

"I used to be a hockey player. I was pretty good even. But I've got a new normal now, and I can't play hockey."

My dad looks down at his lap.

"I used to have a car," I say, "but I sold it. I had to sell it to pay for the damage I did to someone else. But I don't want to drive, not really. I'm afraid to drive. I'm afraid I'll forget what exit to take and that I'll get lost.

I'm afraid I'll have a seizure and drive into someone. My mother takes time off work and drives me to physio appointments and medical appointments." I swallow. "Every day is a personal best, just because I get through it."

I look at the back of the courtroom, at the line of kids standing because there are no seats. I say, "I used to have a best friend. At Riley Park, I lost him. He died in the hospital."

I look at Darius's mother. She blinks back tears.

"But that's where I lost him, at Riley Park. That's where he was when he was last alive. He and I, we jumped the gap and he was alive." I point at the kids at the back of the room. "At Riley Park, we all lost Darius."

I look again at Quinton. "I almost died at Riley Park. Not when Quinton hit me in the back of the head with the bar, although part of me died that night. But I broke through the ice at Riley Park, and a girl saved me. Her name is Rubee."

Quinton looks down.

"None of this is Rubee's fault, but she felt she had to move away. She'll graduate with a bunch of people she doesn't even know. And she lost Darius too. Quinton didn't own Rubee. He tried, but she's better than that."

I turn to Officer Rex. I say, "I used to fight because it made me feel strong. Now I fight for my strength."

I extend my hand. He smiles, and I notice the splint is gone from his teeth. He takes my hand and shakes it.

Finally, I turn back to the judge. "Every day I fight what happened to me. It's supposed to get easier, but I don't see it getting easier, not yet. I don't know who I am, not yet. All I know is what happened to me isn't who I am. I don't know if that even makes sense."

The judge leans forward. "You're doing fine," she says.

"Yes." I take a big breath. "Maybe I am."

Diane Tullson is the best-selling author of *Red Sea*, *Saving Jasey*, *The Darwin Expedition* and *Lockdown*. Diane lives in Delta, British Columbia, and is working on an MFA at the University of British Columbia.